14.95

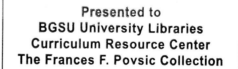

Crow Made a Friend

MARGARET PEOT

Holiday House / New York

For Mom and Dad

I LIKE TO READ is a registered trademark of Holiday House, Inc.

Copyright © 2015 by Margaret Peot
All Rights Reserved
HOLIDAY HOUSE is registered in the U.S. Patent and Trademark Office.
Printed and Bound in April 2015 at Tien Wah Press, Johor Bahru, Johor, Malaysia.
The artwork was created with pen and ink and watercolors.
www.holidayhouse.com
First Edition
1 3 5 7 9 10 8 6 4 2

Library of Congress Cataloging-in-Publication Data
Peot, Margaret. author, illustrator.
Crow made a friend / Margaret Peot. — First edition.
pages cm — (I like to read)
Summary: A lonely crow tries to make a friend
from sticks and leaves, then from snow,
before forming a friendship that will last.
ISBN 978-0-8234-3297-4 (hardcover)
[1. Friendship—Fiction.
2. Crows—Fiction.] I. Title.
PZ7.P397Cro 2014
[E]—dc23
2014024929

ISBN 978-0-8234-3420-6 (paperback)

Crow is alone.

He has a plan. He uses sticks.

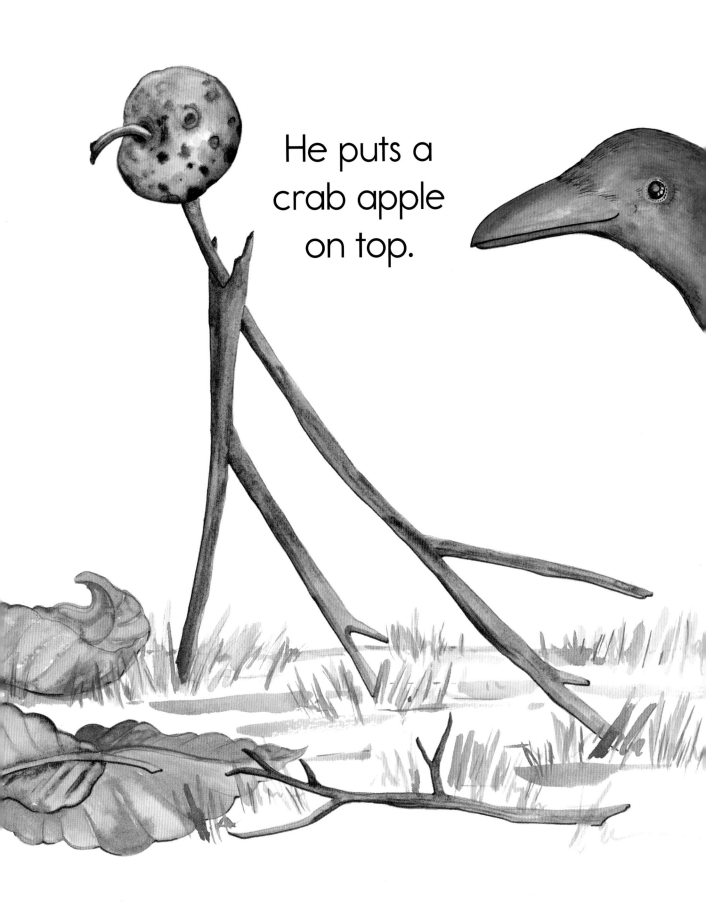

He puts a
crab apple
on top.

Leaves make wings.

Crow made a friend.

The wind blows.

Oh no!

Crow is alone again.

He has a new plan.

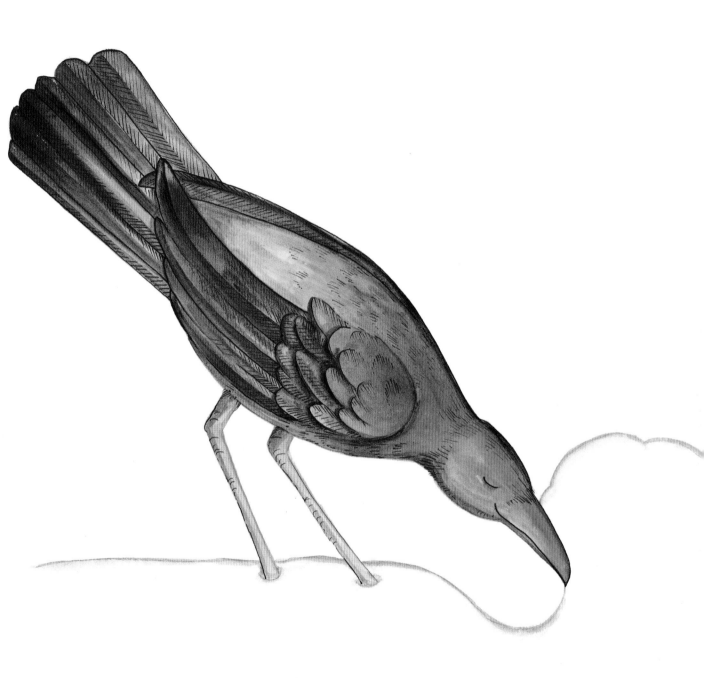

He piles the snow. He pats it.

He puts in a seed.

Sticks make wings.

Crow made a new friend.

The sun shines.

Oh no!

Crow is alone again.

A bird calls.
Caw   Caw   Caw

Crow made a new friend.

They have
a plan.

They use sticks
to make a nest.

Now Crow has a family.